Looking for Leprechauns

For my darling Kevin—S.K.

For my leprechauns: Peter, Alex, and Andrew—P.M.

ISBN 0-439-68057-3

Text copyright © 2005 by Sheila Keenan
Illustrations copyright © 2005 by Paul Meisel
All rights reserved. Published by Scholastic Inc.
SCHOLASTIC and associated logos are trademarks
and/or registered trademarks of Scholastic Inc.

12 11 10 9   9 10/0

Printed in the U.S.A.
First printing, February 2005

Book design by Janet Kusmierski

Looking for Leprechauns

by Sheila Keenan
illustrated by Paul Meisel

SCHOLASTIC INC.
New York Toronto London Auckland Sydney
Mexico City New Delhi Hong Kong Buenos Aires

Kevin and Devin lived with their grandmother
in a little white cottage on the edge of town.
They loved their granny and she loved them.
But there was something else the brothers loved, too — mischief!

Kevin and Devin were always up to something.
They built a tower out of potatoes
and turned the scarecrow upside down.

They played ghosts in the washing.

They put hats on the horses and taught the dogs to sing.

And every night they made monkey faces at the dinner table.
"Stop that nonsense!" their granny said, though she did laugh.

One fine morning, Devin said to Kevin,
"Let's look for leprechauns."
"Why?" asked Kevin.

"Don't you remember Granny's stories?" said Devin.
"A leprechaun has a big pot of gold. If you catch him, it's yours.
All you have to do is make him laugh first."

Kevin thought about all the things he could do with a big pot of gold.
"You're right," he told Devin. "Let's look for leprechauns!"
The brothers found an old wooden cart.
They threw a big kettle with a lid, a long rope,
and a butterfly net into the cart.
"This stuff will help us catch a leprechaun. Ready?" asked Devin.
"Ready!" said Kevin.

Kevin pushed the cart.
Devin pulled it.
When the road dipped down, Devin said, "Let's ride!"
The two brothers hopped into the cart.
It started rolling,
and rolling,
and rolling...
"Look out!" shouted Kevin.

The cart with the kettle,
the rope,
the butterfly net,
and the two boys
rolled right under a fence.
It rumbled through a field
and ran smack into a tree.

The tree shook!
The cart tipped over.
Kevin was tangled up in the rope.
Devin was caught in the butterfly net.
THUNK!

Something landed in the kettle!

The pot started rattling.
"Grrhmph! Let me out! Grrrmph!"
Kevin grabbed the lid and held it tight.
Devin peeked in.
"It's a leprechaun!" he cried.

He reached into the pot and pulled out
the wee man by his coattails.
"We've caught a leprechaun!"

"Put me down!" cried the leprechaun.
"Can't a leprechaun take a nap without being disturbed?"
Devin put the wee man down on the ground.
The leprechaun was hopping mad.
He jumped up and down.
He shook his fist.
He puffed up his cheeks and his face turned red.

"What about the gold?" Kevin whispered to his brother. "How will we ever make him laugh *now*?"

Devin stared at Kevin.
The rope hung off Kevin like a long tail, with leaves and branches stuck in it.
"You look really silly," he said.
Kevin looked at Devin.
The butterfly net covered Devin's head and his hair stuck up out of its little holes.
"You should see yourself," Kevin said.
The two boys started making monkey faces at each other.

They danced around and around, making monkey faces.
They made sideways monkey faces,
upside-down monkey faces,
and monkey faces between their knees.

The leprechaun stopped shaking his fists.
His mouth started twitching.
His lips began to curl into a smile.
"Look!" cried Kevin.
"Don't stop!" cried Devin.
The boys went wild making monkey faces.

And then it happened . . .

The leprechaun started laughing!
"Monkey faces!" he howled and slapped his knees.
"We made you laugh! Can we have our gold now?"
asked Devin.
"Please?" added Kevin.

So the leprechaun led them straight to his pot of gold...
and he never stopped laughing the whole way there!